JUNIOR DETECTIVES

CASE FILES OF JACOB & LIAM

THE CASE OF THE MISSING MARBLES
BOOK 1

ROWENA GREFALDA

For my boys.
Your endless curiosity, boundless imagination, and unwavering sense of adventure inspire me daily. This book is for you to remind you to always seek out mysteries, ask questions, and explore the wonders around you.

"The important thing is not to stop questioning. Curiosity has its own reason for existing."

ALBERT EINSTEIN

CONTENTS

INTRODUCTION

In the charming town of Willowbrook, where every street is lined with cozy houses and friendly neighbors, two young boys stand out for their sharp eyes and curious minds. Meet Jacob and Liam, the dynamic duo of the J&L Junior Detective Agency. Armed with magnifying glasses, notebooks, and a keen sense of adventure, these brothers are always looking for mysteries to solve.

Jacob, the older brother, is ten years old and has a natural talent for solving puzzles. With his analytical mind and love for detective novels, he's always ready to crack a case. Liam, at five, brings his boundless energy and imaginative thinking to the team. While he might be younger, his knack for noticing the little things often leads to big breakthroughs.

Together, Jacob and Liam navigate the mysteries of their small town, using their unique skills to uncover the truth. Whether it's a missing cat or a school prank gone wrong, no case is too small—or too big—for these junior detectives. Join them on their latest adventure as they take on their most challenging case yet: the mystery of the missing marbles. It's a story full of twists, turns, and surprising discoveries, all set against the backdrop of a lively school community and the warmth of a close-knit town. Get ready to embark on a journey of fun and mystery with Jacob and Liam, the best junior detectives around!

CHAPTER 1
THE GREAT COOKIE CAPER

I t was a bright and sunny morning in the small town of Willowbrook. Birds chirped happily, and the scent of blooming flowers filled the air. Inside a cozy little house on Maple Street, two brothers, Jacob and Liam, were getting ready for another exciting day.

Jacob, the older brother at ten years old, was sitting on his bed, deeply engrossed in a detective book. He loved reading about mysteries and imagining himself as a great detective. His hair was messy from sleep, and his brown eyes sparkled with curiosity.

Liam, the younger brother, was only five but full of energy and imagination. He was playing with his favorite toy cars on the floor. His hair was tousled, and his brown eyes shone excitedly as he made car noises.

Suddenly, their mom called from the kitchen. "Jacob! Liam! Can you come here for a minute?"

The boys jumped up and ran to the kitchen, wondering what their mom needed. She was standing by the counter, holding an empty cookie jar with a puzzled expression.

"Alright, boys," she said with a hint of a smile. "Who took the last cookie?"

Liam's eyes went wide, and he quickly shook his head. "It wasn't me, Mom! I promise!"

Jacob put on his most serious face, like the detectives in his books. "Let's investigate," he declared, grabbing a magnifying glass from the counter. He peered into the empty cookie jar, looking for clues.

"Hmm," Jacob muttered, inspecting the jar. "No crumbs left behind. The culprit must be very careful."

Liam giggled, trying to stifle a smile. "Maybe it was a cookie-loving ghost!"

Their mom's eyes twinkled as she noticed a small crumb on Liam's shirt. She raised an eyebrow, and Jacob's gaze followed. He grinned and pointed. "Aha! A clue!"

Liam looked down and saw the crumb. He blushed and started laughing. "Oops! I guess I left some evidence!"

Their mom chuckled. "So, the mystery of the missing cookie is solved. The culprit is... Liam!"

Liam grinned sheepishly. "Okay, okay, I ate it! But it was just so yummy!"

Jacob and their mom laughed, and she ruffled Liam's hair. "Well, detective, you did a good job solving the case," she told Jacob.

Jacob puffed up his chest proudly. "It was a team effort," he said, glancing at Liam, who nodded in agreement.

Their mom smiled warmly. "You boys are quite the detectives. Maybe you should start your own detective agency."

Jacob's eyes lit up at the idea. "That's a great idea, Mom! We could solve mysteries and help people!"

Liam jumped up and down with excitement. "Yeah! We can be the best detectives ever!"

Their mom laughed. "Well, you two have fun with that. Just remember, no real mysteries without asking me first, okay?"

The boys nodded eagerly. "We promise!" they chorused.

CHAPTER 2
J&L JUNIOR DETECTIVE AGENCY

After breakfast, Jacob and Liam ran outside to their backyard. They had a giant, sturdy treehouse that their mom had helped them build last summer. It was their favorite place to play and imagine all sorts of adventures. It was the perfect place to set up their detective agency.

Jacob grabbed a piece of cardboard and a marker. He

carefully wrote "J&L Junior Detective Agency" on it and taped it to the treehouse door. Liam watched, his eyes shining with excitement.

Inside the treehouse, they arranged their detective supplies. Jacob had a notebook for taking notes, a flashlight, and a map of Willowbrook. Liam brought his magnifying glass, a toy walkie-talkie, and a bag of snacks – just in case they got hungry during a stakeout.

Jacob sat down at the small table they had set up and looked around. "This is perfect," he said, satisfied. "Our very own detective headquarters."

Liam sat down across from him. "So, what's our first case, Detective Jacob?"

Jacob thought for a moment. "Well, we need a mystery to solve. Let's think... Maybe we can help someone find something they've lost or figure out who's been leaving those strange notes on the bulletin board at school."

Just then, their neighbor, Mrs. Green, appeared at the gate. She looked worried and called out to the boys. "Jacob, Liam! I need your help!"

The boys rushed down the ladder and ran over to the fence. Mrs. Green's face was pale, and she looked very upset.

"What's wrong, Mrs. Green?" Jacob asked, concerned.

Mrs. Green wrung her hands. "It's Mr. Whiskers! He's missing! I can't find him anywhere!"

Liam gasped. "Mr. Whiskers is missing? That's terrible!"

Jacob nodded. "Don't worry, Mrs. Green. The J&L Junior Detective Agency will find him!"

Mrs. Green looked relieved. "Oh, thank you, boys! He's been gone since this morning. He usually returns for breakfast, but I haven't seen him all day."

Jacob pulled out his notebook and started writing. "Okay, we'll need to ask you some questions. When was the last time you saw him?"

Mrs. Green thought for a moment. "Last night, around bedtime. He was curled up on the couch."

"And where have you looked so far?" Jacob continued.

"I've checked the house, the garden, and even the neighbor's yard. But there's no sign of him," Mrs. Green replied, her voice trembling.

Liam nodded seriously. "Don't worry, Mrs. Green. We'll find Mr. Whiskers. He couldn't have gone far."

The boys thanked Mrs. Green and headed back to their treehouse to plan their search. Jacob spread out the map of Willowbrook and circled the areas they needed to check: Mrs. Green's garden, the nearby park, and the alley behind the houses.

Liam picked up the toy walkie-talkie and pretended to talk into it. "Detective Liam to Detective Jacob. Do you copy? Ready to find Mr. Whiskers!"

Jacob chuckled. "Roger that, Detective Liam. Let's go!"

CHAPTER 3
THE CASE OF THE MISSING CAT

They started their search in Mrs. Green's garden. Jacob carefully looked under the bushes while Liam crawled on his hands and knees, peering into every nook and cranny.

After a few minutes, Liam shouted, "Jacob, I found something!"

Jacob hurried over and saw Liam holding a small ball

of orange fur. "This must be from Mr. Whiskers!" Jacob said, examining the fur. "He was here recently."

Next, they checked the alley behind the houses. It was a narrow space with lots of hiding spots. Jacob and Liam split up, each searching one side of the alley. They called out Mr. Whiskers' name, hoping the cat would come out.

"Here, kitty kitty!" Liam called, peeking under a stack of old boxes.

But there was no sign of Mr. Whiskers.

Feeling a bit discouraged, the boys made their way to the park. It was a popular spot for kids and pets, with plenty of places for a cat to hide. They walked along the paths, calling for Mr. Whiskers and asking people if they'd seen him.

As they rounded a corner, Liam suddenly stopped and pointed. "Jacob, look!"

Mr. Whiskers was sitting on a bench, calmly licking his paw. The boys' faces lit up with relief and joy.

"Mr. Whiskers!" Jacob called, running over. The cat looked up, meowed, and jumped down from the bench. He trotted over to the boys, purring loudly.

Liam gently picked him up, cuddling the soft, orange cat. "We found you!" he said, grinning from ear to ear.

The boys quickly made their way back to Mrs. Green's house. She was waiting anxiously by the gate, and her face lit up when she saw them with Mr. Whiskers.

"Oh, thank goodness!" she exclaimed, rushing over. She took Mr. Whiskers from Liam and hugged him close. "Thank you, boys! You're real detectives!"

Jacob smiled proudly. "Just doing our job, Mrs. Green. We're happy to help."

Liam nodded, still smiling. "Yeah, we love solving mysteries!"

Mrs. Green thanked them again and gave them each a big hug. The boys waved goodbye and returned to their treehouse, feeling like true detectives.

As they climbed up the ladder, Jacob turned to Liam. "That was our first official case," he said, smiling. "The J&L Junior Detective Agency is off to a great start!"

Liam nodded enthusiastically. "Yeah! And we found Mr. Whiskers! I can't wait for our next mystery!"

They sat down in their treehouse, still buzzing with excitement. They had solved their first case and helped a neighbor in need. Jacob knew that more mysteries would come their way, and he couldn't wait to solve them with Liam by his side.

And so, the J&L Junior Detective Agency was officially open for business. Jacob and Liam were ready for any mystery that came their way, big or small. They knew they could solve anything with their detective skills and teamwork.

As they sat together in their treehouse, the sun shining down on their little headquarters, the boys couldn't help but smile. This was just the beginning of their detective adventures, and they were ready for whatever came next.

CHAPTER 4
THE MYSTERY AT WILLOWBROOK ELEMENTARY

The sun shone brightly over Willowbrook Elementary, casting a warm glow on the schoolyard. The annual Marble Day competition is just a week away, and every student eagerly anticipated this big event. The competition was epic, with kids bringing their most beautiful and rare marbles to show off and compete in friendly games. However, the true highlight was the school's prized marble collection, a set of unique marbles donated by previous students who donated their winning marbles.

The brothers walked through the school gates, excited about the marble competition. Preparations for the big event were well underway. Jacob was eager to see all the different marbles on display, while Liam couldn't wait to cheer for his favorite players. The anticipation of the big event filled them with energy and excitement.

"I can't wait to see the marbles!" Liam exclaimed, practically bouncing with each step.

"Me neither," Jacob agreed, his eyes shining with anticipation. "I've heard there's even a marble as old as the school. It's called the 'Golden Swirl' and it's supposed to be amazing."

The boys rushed to the main hallway, where the school set up the marble display case. The hallway was full of students excited to see the famous collection. As they made their way through the crowd, they noticed the hushed whispers and worried looks instead of the usual chatter.

"What's happening?" Liam asked, pulling on Jacob's sleeve. He went from excited to confused.

Jacob felt a knot forming in his stomach. Something wasn't right. When they reached the front of the crowd, they both gasped. Beautiful marbles usually fill the glass display case. Today, it was empty. The marbles were gone.

"No way," Jacob murmured, staring at the open case in disbelief. "Where are the marbles?"

Liam's eyes darted around the room. "Maybe someone moved them? Or maybe it's a prank?"

Before they could speculate further, Ms. Johnson, the principal, stepped forward. She was tall with kind eyes, but today, worry lined her face. She addressed the crowd, trying to maintain calm.

"Everyone, please stay calm," Ms. Johnson said, her voice steady but concerned. "It appears the marbles are missing. If anyone has any information, please come forward."

The students exchanged uneasy glances. The prized marbles were not just valuable; they were a cherished part of the school's history. Jacob felt a surge of determination. This was no ordinary problem—it was a mystery, and he and Liam were just the detectives to solve it.

Jacob leaned over to Liam and whispered, "We should help Ms. Johnson. This is a job for the J&L Junior Detective Agency."

Liam nodded, his eyes wide with excitement. "Yeah! We can find the marbles!"

The boys approached Ms. Johnson, who was talking to a group of teachers. She looked over as they came up, her expression softening slightly.

"Ms. Johnson," Jacob began, "we'd like to help find the marbles. We're junior detectives, and we're good at solving mysteries."

Ms. Johnson sighed and nodded. "Thank you, boys. We could use all the help we can get. But please be careful.

This is very serious. Those marbles are a valuable part of our school's history."

Jacob nodded firmly. "We understand. We'll do our best."

Ms. Johnson gave them a small smile. "I know you will. Good luck."

CHAPTER 5
THE INVESTIGATION BEGINS

J acob and Liam didn't waste any time. They knew
solving a mystery meant diving right in, so they
hurried to the scene—the empty display case. The
hallway, usually buzzing with students, was oddly
quiet. It felt like the whole school was holding its breath,
waiting for the mystery to be solved. The glass door of the

case was slightly open as if someone had forgotten to close it properly. The shelves, where colorful, shiny marbles should have been, were bare. It was almost eerie how empty it looked as if something was missing from the heart of the school.

"Let's start by checking out the display case," Jacob said, his voice filled with determination. He crouched down to look closer, scanning the floor for clues. There were no signs of forced entry—no broken glass, no scratches on the lock. Everything looked untouched except for the missing marbles. It was as if they had vanished into thin air.

Liam stood beside him, eyes wide with anticipation. "Do you see anything, Jacob?" he asked, his voice a mix of excitement and worry.

Jacob shook his head first, then suddenly, his eyes caught something shiny near the janitor's closet door next to the display case. He reached out and picked it up, holding it to the light. It was a small, round marble with a swirl of blue and green inside. It looked just like one of the marbles from the missing collection.

"Look at this," Jacob said, showing Liam the marble. It's one of the missing marbles! Do you think the thief dropped it?"

Liam's eyes widened in surprise. "Maybe," he said, leaning in to look closer. "Or it could have rolled away when they opened the case. Either way, it's a clue."

Jacob nodded, turning the marble over in his hand.

"Yeah, it's a clue," he agreed. He carefully put the marble in his pocket, treating it like precious evidence. "Let's check the janitor's closet next. Maybe something in there can help us figure out what happened."

The boys walked over to the closet door and knocked. They waited momentarily, and the door opened, revealing Mr. Brown, the school's janitor. He was a tall man with graying hair and a kind face. He was always friendly and chatty with everyone, often seen whistling as he worked.

"Hello, boys," Mr. Brown greeted them warmly. "Do you Need something cleaned?"

Jacob hesitated for a moment, then took a deep breath. He knew they had to ask the right questions to solve this mystery. "Mr. Brown, we're investigating the missing marbles from the display case," he began. Did you see anything unusual this morning?"

Mr. Brown's expression turned serious. He seemed genuinely concerned as he thought back. "No, I didn't," he said, shaking his head slowly. "I cleaned the gym for most of the morning, preparing it for Marble Day. Why do you ask?"

Liam couldn't hold back any longer. "The marbles are gone!" he exclaimed, his voice filled with worry. "We're trying to find out what happened to them."

Mr. Brown's eyes widened in shock. "Gone? Oh, that's terrible!" he said, looking around as if he could somehow spot the missing marbles in the hallway. "Those marbles are a part of our school's history. They've been here for as long as I can remember." He sighed, rubbing the back of his neck. "I didn't see anything odd, but I'll watch. I'll let you know immediately if I notice anything suspicious."

Jacob nodded, appreciating Mr. Brown's willingness to help. "Thanks, Mr. Brown. We'll keep looking for clues," he said, hopeful and frustrated. They had found a clue but were still far from solving the mystery.

As they walked away from the janitor's closet, Liam tugged on Jacob's sleeve. He glanced back at the closet door, then looked up at his brother with a worried expression. "Do you think Mr. Brown could have taken the marbles?" he whispered as if speaking too loudly might make it accurate.

Jacob shook his head, deep in thought. "I don't think so," he said thoughtfully. "He seemed genuinely surprised when we told him the marbles were missing. And he's always been nice to everyone. But we can't rule anyone out yet. We must consider all possibilities, even the ones that seem unlikely."

Liam nodded, still looking unsure. "Yeah, but Mr. Brown has always been so kind. It's hard to imagine him doing something like this.".

As Jacob and Liam walked down the hallway, Jacob couldn't shake the feeling that something important was slipping through their fingers. They had found a marble and talked to Mr. Brown, but they still had no real clues. The hallway seemed strangely quiet, and it felt like everyone was aware of the missing marbles. The emptiness in the display case echoed through the entire school, reminding them of the mystery they still had to solve.

"We need to find more clues," Jacob said, more to himself than to Liam. "We can't just rely on what people tell us. We must look deeper and find the details everyone else is missing."

Liam nodded, his face serious. "Yeah, like real detectives," he agreed, trying to sound confident. "We'll figure this out, Jacob. We just have to keep looking."

Jacob smiled at his brother's determination. Even though Liam was younger, he had a sharp eye for details and a never-give-up attitude. Together, they made a great team. They had previously solved more minor mysteries, but this was their biggest challenge yet.

They walked through the school, keeping their eyes open for anything strange. The school was enormous, with many places where someone could hide something. As they passed by the cafeteria, they heard the sound of trays clattering and people talking. Everything seemed normal, but Jacob knew they couldn't take things at face value.

They headed outside to the playground, where kids were chatting and unaware of the missing marbles. The sun shone, and laughter and shouts filled the air. It seemed like an ordinary day, but for Jacob and Liam, the mystery was still on their minds.

"Could someone have hidden the marbles somewhere around here?" Liam asked, looking around the playground.

Jacob shrugged. "It's possible. But we need to find more clues first. We can't just start searching randomly. We need a plan."

Liam nodded, his eyes scanning the playground. "Let's talk to more people. Maybe someone saw something they didn't realize was important."

Jacob agreed. They walked over to a group of kids sitting on the swings, eating snacks and chatting. It was time to gather more information and find the clue that would break the case wide open.

As they approached the group, Jacob took a deep breath. He knew that asking the right questions was necessary to get the answers they needed. "Hey, guys," he called out, sounding casual. Did anyone see anything weird this morning? Anything at all?"

The group quieted down, turning their attention to Jacob and Liam. A girl named Emma raised her hand hesitantly. She was a bit older than Jacob. Emma was known for being quiet but very observant. She had a reputation for noticing details others often missed, and today was no different.

"I heard a strange noise coming from the hallway," she said softly, her voice barely above a whisper. "It sounded like marbles clinking together."

Jacob's eyes widened. This was the first solid lead they had. He quickly pulled out his detective notebook and jotted down what Emma said. "What time was that?" he asked, looking up from his notes.

Emma thought for a moment, her brow furrowing in concentration. "It was before the first bell, around 8:00 AM, I think."

Jacob nodded, scribbling in his notebook. "Thanks, Emma. That's helpful."

As Jacob was writing, another student, Max, stepped forward, eager to share his knowledge. Max was a lively boy, always in the middle of things. "I saw Tim hanging around the display case earlier," he exclaimed. "He looked nervous."

Jacob and Liam exchanged knowing glances. Tim had a reputation for pulling pranks and getting into trouble. He was known for being mischievous, and the idea of him messing with the marbles didn't seem far-fetched. He could be a suspect.

"Where did you see him?" Liam asked, leaning in with interest.

Max pointed towards the front of the school. "Right by the display case. He was just standing there, looking around, like he was up to something."

Jacob and Liam thanked the group for this new information and decided to find Tim. They spotted him sitting alone on a bench near the playground, fiddling with a yo-yo. His head was down, and he seemed lost in thought or trying to avoid attention.

Jacob approached him first, with Liam following close behind. "Hey, Tim," Jacob said, trying to keep his voice light and friendly, not wanting to scare him off. "Did you see anything strange this morning? Around the display case?"

Tim looked up, and for a moment, his eyes darted around nervously. He shrugged, not meeting their gaze.

"Nope. Just walked by like everyone else," he mumbled, focusing intently on the yo-yo in his hands.

Liam squinted at him, sensing something was off. He wasn't convinced. "Some people said you looked nervous. Do you know anything about the missing marbles?" he pressed, his tone gentle but curious.

Tim's face turned red, and he fidgeted with his yo-yo even more. He was uncomfortable, which made Jacob and Liam even more suspicious. "I didn't take them if that's what you're thinking!" Tim exclaimed, his voice rising slightly. "I was just... I don't know... I was just hanging around," he stammered, struggling to explain himself.

Jacob noticed Tim's fidgeting and mysterious gaze. Something felt off, but they couldn't accuse him outright without concrete evidence. Tim's nervous behavior could mean many things, but it wasn't enough to prove he had anything to do with the missing marbles.

"Okay, Tim," Jacob said, keeping his voice calm and even, trying not to sound accusatory. "But if you remember anything, let us know. We're trying to find the marbles before the competition starts."

Tim nodded and looked away, still fiddling with his yo-yo, clearly uncomfortable and perhaps even a little scared. It was hard to tell if he was hiding something or just nervous because he was being questioned. Either way, Jacob and Liam knew they couldn't ignore the possibility that Tim might know more than he was letting on.

As they walked away, Jacob and Liam shared a look. They didn't have enough to go on yet, but they were definitely onto something. The missing marbles were still out there, and they were determined to find them. They had gathered some valuable information, but the mystery was far from solved. The day wasn't over, and neither was their investigation. They just needed to keep digging and find the truth.

CHAPTER 6
THE HOODED FIGURE

After talking to Tim, the boys checked the school's security cameras. They headed to the office, where Ms. Johnson allowed them to review the footage. The video showed students arriving, teachers setting up, and the usual morning bustle. But then, around 7:45 AM, they spotted something unusual.

A figure in a hoodie walked down the hallway near the

display case. The person was careful not to show their face, keeping their head down and hands in their pockets. The figure briefly paused by the display case, then quickly disappeared from view.

"Who do you think it is?" Liam asked, squinting at the screen, trying to make out any details.

Jacob shook his head, frustrated. "I can't tell. The hoodie makes it hard to see. But this person might know something about the missing marbles."

They continued to watch the footage, hoping to catch another glimpse of the figure, but they couldn't find any valuable clues. The boys thanked Ms. Johnson and left the office excitedly and frustrated. They had a potential suspect, but they still needed more information.

The schoolyard was filled with kids eating, playing, and talking about the missing marbles as lunchtime approached. Jacob and Liam sat on a bench, reviewing their notes and trying to piece everything together.

"Okay," Jacob began, tapping his pencil on his notebook. "We have a stray marble found near the janitor's closet, a strange noise around 8:00 AM, and a figure in a hoodie on the security footage. Tim is also acting weird and not telling us the whole truth."

Liam nodded, taking a big bite of his sandwich. "Mr. Brown said he didn't see anything, but he could've missed something while cleaning."

Jacob sighed, feeling the weight of the mystery. "We need to figure out who was wearing that hoodie. Maybe someone saw them and can tell us more."

CHAPTER 7
THE CHIPPED MARBLE

Jacob and Liam decided to head back to their treehouse to review their notes and determine their next steps. However, as they walked across the playground, they noticed Eric standing by the old jungle gym, talking to a few students. He seemed to be showing them something.

Curious, Jacob and Liam approached the group. Eric noticed them and grinned mischievously. "Hey, detectives! You're just in time," he called out, holding up a shiny marble.

Jacob's eyes narrowed. The marble looked just like the ones from the missing collection. "What's going on, Eric?" he asked cautiously.

Eric tossed the marble in the air and caught it with a flourish. "I found this behind the art room," he said. "I think it's one of the missing marbles. Maybe the thief dropped it."

Liam leaned in closer, examining the marble. "It looks just like the others," he said, eyes wide with excitement. "Do you think there's more?"

Eric shrugged, his grin widening. "Maybe. If there's one, there could be others, right? We should check it out."

Jacob felt a familiar sense of caution. Something didn't feel right about this. "Mind if we take a closer look at that marble?" he asked, reaching out his hand.

Eric hesitated for a moment, then handed it over. "Sure, go ahead," he said casually.

Jacob inspected the marble carefully. It was shiny and looked identical to the ones in the missing collection. But as he turned it over in his hand, he noticed a tiny chip on the surface. Something about it seemed off, but he couldn't quite put his finger on it.

"We should go check behind the art room," Liam suggested, already turning to leave. "Maybe we can find more marbles!"

Eric's eyes sparkled with mischief. "Yeah, let's go on a marble hunt," he encouraged, clearly enjoying the attention.

Jacob paused, thinking quickly. "Hold on," he said, looking at Eric. "Are you sure you found this behind the art room?"

Eric blinked, caught off guard. "Uh, yeah. That's what I said," he replied, a hint of defensiveness in his voice.

Jacob frowned, his suspicions growing. "Because I remember you were playing marbles with some of the younger kids during recess last week," he said slowly. "And one of the marbles had a chip just like this one."

Liam's eyes widened as he caught on. "You mean... this isn't from the missing collection?" he asked, turning to Eric.

Eric's grin faltered. "Well, I mean... it's still a marble, right?" he said, trying to brush it off. "It could still be a clue."

Jacob shook his head, feeling a mix of relief and annoyance. "Nice try, Eric," he said, returning the marble. "But this isn't from the missing collection. You just wanted to mess with us."

The other students started to murmur, realizing what had happened. Eric's face turned red, and he looked down, clearly embarrassed. "Okay, fine. You got me," he admitted, rubbing the back of his neck. "I thought it would be funny to see if you guys would fall for it."

Liam frowned. "Why would you do that? We're trying to solve a real mystery here," he said, sounding more hurt than angry.

Eric sighed, looking genuinely apologetic. "I don't know. I guess I just wanted to have a little fun," he said. "I didn't think it would be a big deal."

Jacob took a deep breath, trying to keep his cool. "Next time, think before you do something like this," he said firmly. "We need to focus on finding the real marbles, not chasing fake clues."

Eric nodded, looking sheepish. "Yeah, you're right. I'm sorry, guys. I didn't mean to waste your time."

As Jacob and Liam headed back to their treehouse, Liam sighed. "I can't believe he did that. We almost thought we found a real clue."

Jacob nodded, but he couldn't help but smile a little. "At least we figured it out quickly," he said. "And now we know to be more careful about what clues we follow."

CHAPTER 8
GETTING BACK ON TRACK

Jacob and Liam sat in their treehouse, staring at the clues they had gathered. The sun was setting, casting a warm orange glow through the windows. It had been a long day of investigating, and they were no closer to finding out who had taken the marbles. The usual excitement of solving a mystery was fading, replaced by a creeping feeling of doubt.

Jacob sighed, flipping through his notebook. "We've gone over everything a hundred times," he muttered. We have the marble we found near the janitor's closet, the strange noise at 8 AM, the hooded figure in the security footage, and the weird way Tim acted. But none of it leads us to the thief."

Liam, sitting across from him, nodded slowly. "Yeah, and we asked everyone if they saw anything. But no one knows anything," he said, frustration creeping into his voice. He looked down, fiddling with a pencil. "Maybe... maybe we're not as good at this as we thought."

Jacob looked up, surprised by Liam's words. "What do you mean?" he asked, feeling worried.

Liam shrugged, avoiding Jacob's eyes. "I don't know. We can't even figure out who took the marbles. Maybe we're not real detectives. Maybe we're just pretending."

The words stung. Jacob had always been confident in their abilities, but hearing Liam doubt them made him question everything. He had never seen Liam so unsure before. "Hey, we're doing our best," Jacob said, trying to reassure him. "It's a tough case, but we'll figure it out."

Liam shook his head. "But what if we don't? What if we never find the marbles?" His voice was small, almost a whisper. "What if we fail?"

Jacob felt a knot form in his stomach. He didn't want to admit it, but he was starting to feel the same way. They had hit so many dead ends, and the pressure was getting to him, too. "I... I don't know," he finally said, looking down at his notebook. "But we can't give up now."

Liam sighed, leaning back in his chair. "I guess," he mumbled, not sounding convinced. "But it feels like we're just going in circles."

The room went quiet. The boys sat there, thinking. It felt strange and sad like they had worries they weren't discussing. They had always worked together as a team to solve mysteries, but now it felt like they were drifting apart, each feeling frustrated.

After a few minutes, Liam stood up. "I'm going to get some fresh air," he said abruptly, heading for the door. "Maybe it'll help me think."

Jacob watched Liam leave, feeling a bit worried. He wanted to say something to cheer him up, but he couldn't think of anything. So, he stayed behind, looking at the clues and feeling more alone than ever.

As Liam walked outside, the cool evening air touched his face. He took a big breath, trying to clear his head. The yard was quiet except for the distant sound of crickets. He wandered over to the swings and sat down, gently swinging back and forth. His mind was full of thoughts and worries.

He thought about all the times they had solved mysteries together, like finding the missing cat or figuring out who took the last cookie. Those cases were easier than this one. The missing marbles felt like a puzzle they couldn't solve, making him feel small and unsure.

Meanwhile, Jacob stayed in the treehouse, looking at the clues with a frown. He thought about everything that happened that day, trying to figure out what happened.

Every time they thought they had a clue, it led nowhere. He felt like they had failed, which was hard to shake off.

After a while, Liam came back inside, looking a little calmer. He sat down across from Jacob, who looked up with a worried expression. "Feeling better?" Jacob asked carefully.

Liam nodded, but he still looked unsure. "Yeah, a little," he said. "But I'm still not sure what we're missing."

Jacob sighed and leaned back in his chair. "Me neither," he said quietly. "But maybe... maybe we're looking at this incorrectly."

Liam looked at him, curious. "What do you mean?"

Jacob thought for a moment, trying to explain. "Maybe we're trying too hard to find a big, obvious clue," he said. "Maybe the answer is something small, something we didn't notice."

Liam thought about it and nodded slowly. "Like what?"

"I don't know," Jacob admitted. "But we should go back and look at everything again. Maybe there's a little detail we missed that seemed unimportant."

Liam looked down at the clues on the table. It wasn't much, but it was better than giving up. "Okay," he said finally. "Let's try one more time."

The boys spent the next hour reviewing every clue and piece of information they had. They discussed all the possibilities, trying to see the mystery from different angles. It was hard work, but they started to piece things together.

Finally, Liam looked up with a slight smile. "I think we

can do this," he said, sounding more confident than he had all day. "We just have to keep going."

Jacob nodded and smiled back. "Yeah, we can," he agreed. "We just have to believe in ourselves and each other."

As it got darker, they gathered their clues and went inside. They still had a lot to figure out but felt they were on the right path. Most importantly, they knew they could rely on each other. No matter what, they were a team, and nothing could change that.

CHAPTER 9
TIM AND THE TRUTH

The next day, the boys made their way to the playground. They spotted Tim sitting by himself, still fiddling with his yo-yo. Jacob and Liam approached him cautiously, not wanting to accuse him but hoping to get some answers.

"Hey, Tim," Jacob said, trying to sound casual. "Can we talk to you for a minute?"

Tim looked up nervously. "Uh, sure," he replied, pocketing his yo-yo. "What's up?"

"We just wanted to clear something up," Liam said, trying to sound friendly. "When we talked to you the other day, you seemed nervous. We were wondering if something was bothering you."

Tim hesitated, then sighed. "Okay, I'll tell you the truth," he said, glancing around to ensure no one else was listening. "I wasn't hanging around the display case because of the marbles. I was waiting for my older brother to leave. He works in the school's maintenance crew, and I was supposed to meet him to borrow money. While waiting, I was so nervous that I accidentally bumped into the display case which made a loud noise. I was alarmed because I didn't want anyone to know I was there for the money or that I caused the noise."

Jacob and Liam exchanged glances. Tim's explanation made sense. It explained why he had been so secretive and the strange noise Emma heard around 8 AM.

"So, you weren't involved with the missing marbles?" Jacob asked, just to be sure.

Tim shook his head. "No way. I didn't even know they were missing until you guys told me. I didn't want anyone to find out I was asking my brother for money."

Jacob smiled, relieved. "Thanks for being honest, Tim. That clears things up."

With Tim's confusion cleared up, Jacob and Liam felt a sense of closure. Tim's strange behavior had been a distraction, but now they understood what had happened. He had nothing to do with the missing marbles.

As they walked away, Jacob grinned at Liam. "Well, that explains a lot. Now we can focus on finding the real culprit."

CHAPTER 10
THE BREAKTHROUGH

A s the afternoon wore on, the boys decided to take one last look around the school, hoping to find any overlooked clues. They checked the playground, the gym, and the cafeteria, but nothing seemed unusual. The day was slipping away, and they were running out of time.

Feeling a bit discouraged, they returned to the scene of

the crime—the empty display case. As they stood there, staring at the open glass door, Liam suddenly noticed something.

"Jacob, look!" Liam pointed to a small scratch on the floor near the case. It looked like a fresh scratch.

Jacob crouched down to examine it. "It looks like someone dragged something heavy. Maybe they tried to hide the marbles nearby?"

They followed the scratch marks, which led them back towards the janitor's closet. Jacob felt a surge of excitement. This could be it!

They knocked on the closet door again, and Mr. Brown opened it, looking puzzled. "Back again, boys?" he asked, raising an eyebrow.

"Mr. Brown, we need to check inside the closet again," Jacob said, trying to keep his voice steady. "We think the marbles might be hidden in there."

Mr. Brown looked surprised but stepped aside, opening the door wider. "Of course. Go ahead."

Jacob and Liam carefully searched the closet, moving brooms, mops, and cleaning supplies, checking every nook and cranny. Just when they were about to give up, Liam spotted a small box on a high shelf, partially hidden behind some cleaning supplies.

"Jacob, look!" Liam whispered excitedly, pointing to the box.

Jacob carefully reached up and grabbed the box. He opened it, and the missing marbles shone brightly under the light.

"We found them!" Jacob exclaimed, grinning from ear to ear, feeling a rush of triumph.

Jacob grinned, holding up the box for a closer look. "I can't believe they were here the whole time," he said, shaking his head.

Mr. Brown's eyes widened in realization. "Oh my goodness, I must have put them there while cleaning and completely forgotten about it," he said, shaking his head. "Thank goodness! The marbles are safe. I feel so silly. I'm so sorry for all the trouble this caused." he said, touching his chest.

Liam smiled, relieved. "It's okay, Mr. Brown. We're just glad we found them."

Mr. Brown chuckled, clearly embarrassed. "Well, I'm glad you boys did some good detective work. You've been quite the detectives in solving this mystery."

The boys beamed with pride, feeling like true detectives. They couldn't stop talking about their adventure as they walked out of the closet with Mr. Brown.

Liam nodded. "Yeah, who would've thought it was there? We checked everywhere else!"

Mr. Brown smiled down at them. "You two have a knack for finding things. Maybe you'll be real detectives one day."

As they reached the principal's office, they handed over the box of marbles to Ms. Johnson. She looked relieved and grateful. "Thank you so much, boys. You've saved Marble Day!"

Jacob and Liam grinned, proud of their

accomplishment. "It was a team effort," Jacob said modestly.

Ms. Johnson nodded. "You both did a great job. Now, why don't you enjoy the rest of your day? You've earned it."

As they left the office, the boys felt a sense of accomplishment. They had solved the mystery and found the missing marbles. They knew they made a great team and were ready for whatever mystery came their way next.

Jacob looked at Liam as they walked home and said, "We really did it, huh?"

Liam grinned, his eyes shining with excitement. "Yeah, we did. I can't wait for our next adventure!"

The boys laughed, feeling the thrill of their success. They knew that no matter what, they would always have each other's backs. They were ready for whatever came next, knowing they were a great detective duo.

CHAPTER 11
MARBLE DAY

The day of the Marble Day competition finally arrived, and Willowbrook Elementary was buzzing with excitement. Thanks to Jacob and Liam's hard work, the school's prized marble collection was back in its display case. Colorful banners decorated the gym; kids were everywhere, showing off their marble skills and cheering on their friends.

Jacob and Liam stood near the display case, watching

the festivities. They felt a warm glow of pride, knowing they had helped save the day. As they looked around, Liam turned to Jacob thoughtfully.

"Hey, Jacob," Liam started, "do you remember when we first started this case? We had no idea what we were getting into."

Jacob nodded, smiling. "Yeah, we thought it was just a simple mystery. But it turned out to be a lot more complicated."

Liam laughed. "We made a lot of mistakes, didn't we? Like when we thought Tim was involved just because he acted weird."

Jacob chuckled. "Yeah, we jumped to conclusions a few times. But we learned not to make hasty judgments, right? Just because someone seems suspicious doesn't mean they're guilty."

Liam nodded in agreement. "And we also learned the importance of teamwork. We couldn't have solved the case without working together."

Jacob smiled at Liam. "You're right. We make a great team. And we got better at observing things, like spotting the small box on top of the shelf in the janitor's closet."

Liam grinned. "Yeah, that was a good find. Who knew Mr. Brown accidentally put the marbles there while cleaning?"

They both laughed, remembering the moment they discovered the marbles. It felt good to laugh about it now, knowing they had solved the mystery and learned valuable lessons.

As they watched the Marble Day competition, Jacob felt content. "You know, Liam, this whole experience made us better detectives. We learned to pay attention to the little details and not to overlook anything."

Jacob put his arm around Liam's shoulders, pulling him into a side hug. "I'm glad we did this together," he said warmly. "And I'm proud of us."

Liam beamed up at his brother. "Me too. We make an awesome detective team!"

They stood there for a moment, soaking in the atmosphere of Marble Day. Kids were laughing, marbles were rolling across the floor, and the excitement was contagious. It felt like the perfect ending to their adventure.

"Hey, want to go check out the marble games?" Liam asked, his eyes sparkling with enthusiasm.

Jacob grinned. "Definitely. Let's see if we can win a few rounds."

The brothers joined the other kids, playing games and enjoying the festivities. They laughed, cheered, and celebrated with their friends. It was a day of fun and joy, a reward for their hard work and determination.

As Jacob and Liam continued to enjoy the Marble Day festivities, they spotted a familiar figure. Liam nudged Jacob and pointed towards someone in the crowd. "Hey, there's the hooded figure we kept seeing. We never found out who it was."

Jacob nodded, curious. "Let's find out who it is."

The boys approached the figure, standing alone,

watching the marble games. The figure looked up and gave them a shy smile. "Hey, Jacob and Liam," the boy greeted them, pushing back his hood. "I'm Aidan".

"Hey, Aidan," Jacob said, smiling back. "We noticed you around a lot during our investigation. We thought you might know something about the missing marbles."

Aidan's eyes widened, and he quickly shook his head. "Oh, no, I didn't know anything about that," he said nervously. "I just moved here and didn't want to get in trouble, so I kept to myself."

Liam nodded, understanding. "So, that's why you always wore your hoodie and stayed out of sight?"

Aidan nodded. "Yeah, I was trying to blend in and not draw attention. I didn't want anyone to think I was up to something."

Jacob smiled reassuringly. "We get it. It must be tough being the new kid. Sorry if we made you feel uncomfortable."

Aidan smiled, relieved. "No worries. I'm glad you found the marbles, though. You guys did a great job."

"Thanks," Liam said with a grin. "And hey, if you ever want to hang out or need help with anything, let us know. We're all friends here."

Aidan's face lit up, and he nodded. "That sounds great. Thanks, guys."

With the mystery of the hooded figure cleared up, Jacob and Liam felt even more satisfied with how everything had turned out. They had solved the case, made a new friend, and learned not to judge someone based on appearances.

As they enjoyed the day, they knew they had grown as detectives and people.

As they walked home, Jacob smiled at Liam. "So, what do you think our next case will be?"

Liam grinned, his eyes full of excitement. "Who knows? But whatever it is, we'll solve it together."

Jacob nodded, feeling a strong bond with his brother. "Yeah, we will. No mystery is too big for us."

The boys laughed, feeling ready for whatever adventures awaited them. They knew they could solve any mystery as long as they worked together. And most importantly, they knew their bond as brothers was more vital than ever.

As they reached their house, Jacob looked at Liam and said, "Let's keep being the best detective team ever."

Liam smiled, nodding. "Deal."

And with that, the boys walked into their house, ready for their next adventure. They were detectives, brothers, and best friends; nothing could change that.

JUNIOR DETECTIVE TRAINING

Hey there, future detective! Do you want to be a junior detective just like Jacob and Liam? If you're ready to dive into the exciting world of mystery-solving, you've come to the right place! Welcome to **Detective Training Camp**, where you'll learn all the cool tricks and skills to crack the most challenging cases.

In this section, we've lined up a bunch of fun and exciting challenges for you. Each activity will help you get closer to becoming an expert at solving everyday mysteries.

So, grab your magnifying glass, put on your detective hat, and get started! Whether you're solving puzzles at home or figuring out clues in the great outdoors, you're about to embark on an adventure that'll make you feel like a real detective. Ready? Let's go!

Puzzle 1: The Fruit Mixup

You have three boxes, each labeled with a different fruit: apples, oranges, and mixed (which contains both apples and oranges). However, all the labels are incorrect. If you can only open one box and take out one fruit, how can you correctly label all the boxes?

Puzzle 2: The Light Switches

Behind a door are three light switches on the wall, all in the "off" position. In the adjacent room, there are three light bulbs, each controlled by one of these switches. You can flip the switches however you like, but you may only enter the adjacent room once to check the lights. How can you determine which switch controls which light bulb?

Puzzle 3: Truth-tellers and Liars

In a small village, there are only two types of people: truth-tellers, who always tell the truth, and liars, who always lie. You meet two villagers, Jane and Bob. Janee says, "We are both truth-tellers." Bob says, "Jane is a liar." What are Jane and Bob?

Puzzle 4: The Stolen Necklace

A priceless necklace has been stolen, and the suspects are four individuals: John, Mary, Paul, and Lisa. The following statements were made during the investigation:

- John: "It wasn't me."
- Mary: "It was Paul."
- Paul: "Lisa did it."
- Lisa: "Paul is lying."

If only one of these statements is true, who stole the necklace?

Puzzle 5: Hidden Marbles

Now, let's test your observation skills. The picture above contains seven hidden marbles. Can you find them all?

WELCOME TO THE J&L JUNIOR DETECTIVE AGENCY

You've done an incredible job of solving puzzles, cracking cases, and using your keen observation skills. We are thrilled to present you with your very own **Junior Detective Badge**! This badge symbolizes your hard work, sharp mind, and dedication to uncovering the truth.

Wear it proudly as a reminder of all the mysteries you've unraveled and the adventures you've embarked on. Whether you're solving riddles at home, investigating mysteries with friends, or simply exploring the world, know you're part of an elite team of junior detectives.

Keep up the great work, stay curious, and never stop asking questions. The world is full of mysteries waiting to be solved, and we know you're up to the challenge. Congratulations once again, Junior Detective!

ANSWERS

Puzzle 1: Fruit Mixup

Open the box labeled "Mixed." Since all the labels are wrong, this box can't have apples and oranges. It will only have one type of fruit, either all apples or all oranges.

If you find an apple inside, the box only has apples. So, the box labeled "Apples" must have only oranges, and the box labeled "Oranges" must have both apples and oranges.

If you find an orange inside, the box only has oranges. So, the box labeled "Oranges " must have only apples, and the box labeled "Apples" must have both apples and oranges.

Puzzle 2: The Light Switches

- Turn on the first switch and leave it on for a few minutes.
- Turn off the first switch, turn on the second switch, and then enter the adjacent room.
- The bulb that is on corresponds to the second switch.
- The bulb that is off but warm corresponds to the first switch.
- The bulb that is off and cold corresponds to the third switch.

Puzzle 3: The Truth-tellers and Liars

Jane is a liar, and Bob is a truth-teller.

If Jane were telling the truth (that they are both truth-tellers), Bob's statement (that Jane is a liar) would be false, which contradicts the scenario. Therefore, Jane must be lying, making Bob a truth-teller. Bob's statement that Jane is a liar is then true.

Puzzle 4: The Stolen Necklace

John stole the necklace.

If John's statement is true (John didn't do it):

- If John didn't do it, then Mary, Paul, and Lisa are lying.
- Mary says, "It was Paul," which must be false, so Paul didn't do it.
- Paul says, "Lisa did it," which must be false, so Lisa didn't do it.
- Lisa says, "Paul is lying," which must be false, so Paul is not lying.
- This means Paul is telling the truth, which contradicts our condition that only one statement can be true. Thus, John's statement cannot be true.

If Mary's statement is true (Paul did it):

- If Paul did it, then John, Paul, and Lisa are lying.
- John says, "It wasn't me," which must be false, so John did it.
- Paul says, "Lisa did it," which must be false, so Lisa didn't do it.
- Lisa says, "Paul is lying," which must be false, so Paul is not lying.
- This means Paul is telling the truth, which contradicts the condition that only one statement can be true. Thus, Mary's statement cannot be true.

If Paul's statement is true (Lisa did it):

- If Lisa did it, then John, Mary, and Lisa are lying.
- John says, "It wasn't me," which must be false, so John did it.
- Mary says, "It was Paul," which must be false, so Paul didn't do it.
- Lisa says, "Paul is lying," which must be false, so Paul is not lying.
- This creates a contradiction because if Paul's statement is true, then Lisa did it, but this cannot be true if only one statement is true. Thus, Paul's statement cannot be true.

If Lisa's statement is true (Paul is lying):

- If Paul is lying, then his statement, "Lisa did it," is false, so Lisa didn't do it.
- Since Lisa didn't do it, the thief must be someone else.
- If Lisa's statement is the only true one, then John, Mary, and Paul are lying.
- John says, "It wasn't me," which must be false, so John did it.
- Mary says, "It was Paul," which must be false, so Paul didn't do it.
- Paul's statement, "Lisa did it," is false, confirming that Lisa didn't do it.
- So, if only one statement is true, and that statement is Lisa's, then the thief must be **John**.

Puzzle 5: Hidden Marbles

MESSAGE FROM THE AUTHOR

Hello Junior Detectives,

Thank you for joining Jacob and Liam on their exciting adventure to solve the mystery of the missing marbles. Writing this book has been thrilling, and I'm so glad you could join us.

When I was your age, I loved reading stories about brave detectives who solved mysteries and uncovered secrets. Those stories sparked my imagination and made me want to explore the world. I wanted to create a story where you, the reader, could feel part of the adventure, solving puzzles and discovering hidden clues.

Jacob and Liam were inspired by and named after my two boys, who share the same love for solving mysteries. Like the book's characters, my sons are curious and love to figure out how things work. Their enthusiasm and teamwork were a big inspiration for this story. It's a reminder that anyone can be a detective, no matter how old. All it takes is a curious mind, a keen eye for details, and a willingness to work together.

Jacob and Liam learned that it's essential to keep going and never give up, even when things get tough. They also discovered that sometimes the real treasure isn't just finding the answer but the friendships and memories made along the way.

I hope this story inspires you to embrace your curiosity

and look at the world with a detective's eye. Whether it's solving a minor mystery in your backyard or figuring out how things work, endless wonders are waiting to be explored.

If you enjoyed the adventure and have your own stories or mysteries you'd like to share, I'd love to hear from you. Just scan the QR code below. Keep being curious, asking questions, and, most importantly, having fun!

Happy sleuthing!

Rowena Grefalda

Made in the USA
Columbia, SC
29 November 2024